Tales at the Lake

Book 2
in the
FOX HOLLOW SERIES

Bonnie J. Gibson

Flint Hills Publishing

Original art by the author

GIBSON MADE, LLC

Cover Design by Amy Albright

STONY POINT
Graphics

Flint Hills Publishing
Topeka, Kansas

www.flinthillspublishing.com

Printed in the U.S.A.

ISBN: 978-1-7332035-9-3

DEDICATION

For my golden daughter-in-law, Jessalynn,
and my shining star granddaughter, Emmersyn Rae.

Down in Fox Hollow, Momma Fox's cubs Brush and Meadow were curled up fast asleep. They were dreaming while snowflakes floated down from the sky.

It was winter in Fox Hollow. The trees were bare, the flowers tucked away underground, resting up for spring. The air was light and frosty.

Brush and Meadow loved the winter season. Their fur coats always kept them warm and cozy while they played with other forest friends outside.

Today was especially exciting. Brush and Meadow were going on a lake adventure. The very first frozen lake adventure of the season.

While the cubs were still sleeping, Momma Fox packed their backpacks with yummy snacks and thermoses full of steaming hot apple cider.

It was a good thing Momma Fox had the backpacks ready. When Brush and Meadow awoke, they almost flew out of the house before eating breakfast. Momma Fox could barely get two pancakes rolled up with berry jelly into their paws.

The cubs ran all the way to the lake. When they arrived, they dropped their backpacks on some rocks and immediately started building a snowman.

Soon their turtle friend Gully arrived. Gully loved to hang on to Meadow's tail as the cubs skated all over the icy pond. "Weeeeeee Hooooo!" hollered Gully when his body lifted off the ice.

When it was time to relax and have their snacks, the cubs laid a blanket on the ground behind some large boulders. Gully could not join them. Gully and his pa had plans to work on a new purple kite. It was their favorite hobby to work on together. Since winter was too cold for turtles, they would hunker down for a long winter's nap.

While the cubs rested behind the boulder, there was a rustling of noise coming from nearby. They gathered all their belongings and popped their heads up to see what was happening.

It was girls! "Oh, my goodness," squeaked Meadow. "I wonder if Momma has ever seen real live girls before?"

The cubs remained still as they watched the beautiful creatures float and twirl across the ice.

After the girls left, Brush and Meadow came out from behind the rocks.

"Brush," asked Meadow in her sweet and squeaky voice, "were they the prettiest girls in all of Fox Hollow?"

"Geeze," shrugged Brush, "what does that matter?" And he went about his play.

Meanwhile, Meadow started to feel sad on the inside. She did not understand what she was feeling, she just knew she wanted to cry.

Fortunately, their fawn friends Buck and Blossom arrived. Buck was full of enthusiasm and Blossom was a little shy. "Hi, Buck!" hollered Brush.

"Hi, Meadow!" said Blossom. And Meadow began to feel happier on the inside.

Blossom liked to play outside. But her favorite thing on earth was to read books. Meadow found reading to be a little boring. So, Blossom would read them out loud to Meadow with funny voices to keep it entertaining. Meadow would giggle and that filled Blossom with great joy.

When Blossom talked about all her dreams of someday being a story writer, Meadow began to feel sad again. She was happy for Blossom. But she felt upset because *she* didn't have a dream.

Meadow began to feel her tummy ache. She asked Brush if they could go home. Brush said yes, and the two cubs waived goodbye to their friends.

Brush noticed that Meadow was extra quiet on the way home. He asked her if she felt all right. "I don't know, Brush," squeaked Meadow. "I don't know what's happening to my inside."

"Is it your tummy?" asked Brush.

"No," replied Meadow, "it is a feeling way up high."

At dinner, Momma asked the cubs about their day. Brush could barely take a breath while he shared about all the fun they had at the lake.

When Momma turned to Meadow, Meadow simply squeaked, "It was all right."

"Just all right?" asked Momma.

"Well," said Meadow, "I guess it was better than all right. We built a magnificent snowman and I pulled Gully all over the ice. Blossom read me a lot of stories and her voices gave me the giggles. Oh, and Momma, we saw real live girls."

"What?" asked Momma.

"It's okay," replied Meadow. "Brush and I just hid behind the boulders. Oh, Momma, they were the most beautiful sight. They twirled and floated all over the ice. I sure wish I was that pretty and talented."

Momma took Meadow's cheeks in her hands and said, "My Meadow, you are the kindest and prettiest Meadow that has ever lived." Then Meadow began to cry.

Brush ran over to hug Meadow tight, "And you're the very best sister a cub could ever have." Meadow put her paws on her chest and Momma asked her if she was all right. Meadow told her Momma that she had a tummy ache, way up high.

"Oh, my darling," said Momma, "that's not your tummy, that's your heart."

"Why does her heart ache, Momma?" asked Brush.

"Well," responded Momma, "that's what happens when we only focus on the outside."

"Outside?" questioned Meadow."

"Yes, said Momma, "we can play silly tricks on our mind by over-thinking how someone else is better, smarter, prettier, faster—instead of just knowing that they are good, smart, pretty, and fast. Before we know it, we allow ourselves to believe that we have none of those same qualities. It is telling ourselves lies."

"Lies are bad!" shrieked Meadow.

"That's exactly right," responded Momma. "Remember this, my darlings, when you are dreaming late tonight; the world is full of wonderous shapes and colors that can look different at different times. Just like all the trees in Fox Hollow, we change and grow as seasons pass, becoming wiser every day while seeing through many eyes."

"But I couldn't see what Meadow was feeling," Brush said, "even when I asked her what was wrong."

Momma responded, "We must always try, my darlings, because feelings matter and it is good to talk about them so we can hear another view, since each of us are different, living different lives. If we share our lives together, it opens up our minds. Now, it's time for bed. Let's all snuggle up together and dream about happy new adventures with truthful, open minds."

"Momma," said Meadow half-asleep, "can we say a prayer to ask God to fix my broken heart and untruthful mind?"

"You just did, my darling, by sharing what was on your heart and mind."

Momma stroked their tiny foreheads until they both fell fast asleep and whispered, "I love you."

The End.

About the Author

This story was inspired by my beautiful family who has learned so much from my daughter Taylor who was born with Down Syndrome and a critical, congenital heart defect. After surviving Taylor's early childhood challenges, my family and I are navigating the very unique world of Taylor's adulthood. In this new chapter, I have become joyously aware of the healing power of creativity.

Momma, Bonnie J. Gibson

Taylor Gibson, the author's daughter

Daughter-in-law Jessalynn,
Granddaugher Emmersyn Rae, & son Brenton

The author with her husband, Jeff, & their daughter Taylor

For more about Bonnie and her work:
www.gibsonmade.us
Instagram@lifeacanvas
Facebook: Bonnie J. Gibson Author (@BonnieJGibson)

COMING SOON!

Book 3 in the Fox Hollow Series

Tales of Friendship

Made in the USA
Middletown, DE
02 September 2020